The Knight and the Firefly

a boy, a bug, and a lesson in bravery

Tara McClary Reeves
& Amanda Jenkins

B&H
KIDS

Nashville, Tennessee

In a big green bush, in a not-so-quiet yard,
Phineas the Firefly was taking a nap
when suddenly . . .

He was jolted awake by Doyle—a nasty, smelly bullfrog who lived in a neighboring pond. Day after day, Doyle came crashing into the yard, looking for lunch.

And every day, Oliver the Brave
would be there to stop him.

"Away, frog! Back to the pond
from where you came!"

As long as the sun was shining,
Oliver fought with great courage.

"I am Sir Oliver, frog slayer
and friend to bugs!"

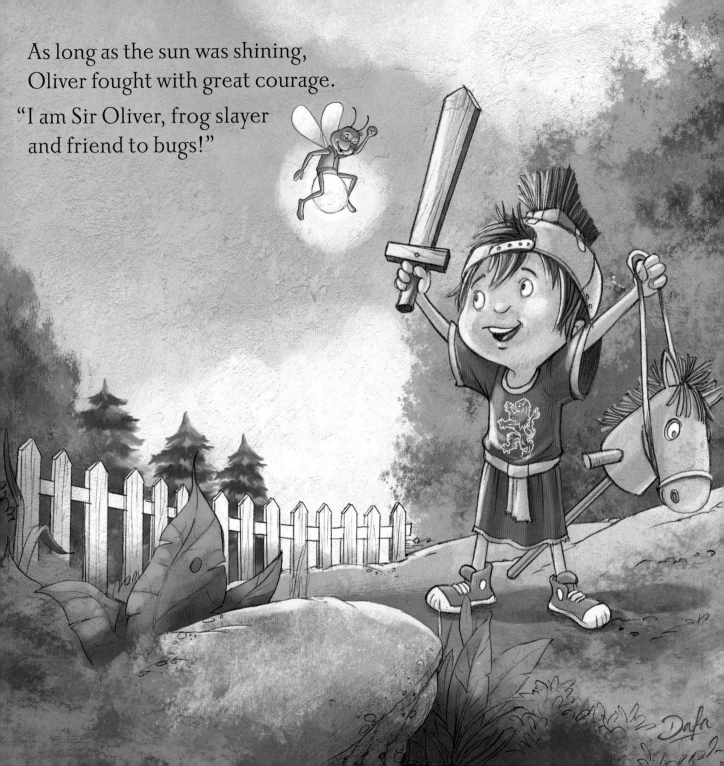

But every night when the sun went down,
Oliver's biggest battle would begin.

"Mom, do dragons have sharp teeth?"

"Mom, are you sure there aren't monsters under here?"

"Oliver," his mother said softly as she tucked him under the covers,
"God *loves* you, and He has the greatest adventure planned for your
life. I want you to trust Him, even when it's dark outside."

Oliver snuggled in close to his mother. He felt safe whenever she
was near.

But alone in his room, the tick-tock of Oliver's clock seemed to get louder and LOUDER as the house got quieter.

And all the scary things that lived in Oliver's imagination kept him awake and afraid.

As soon as the sun came up,
Doyle was back and hungrier than ever.
But this time, the little knight could
not keep up with the wretched frog.
And when Oliver stopped to yawn . . .

Doyle snatched a dragonfly out of the air.

GULP.

BURP.

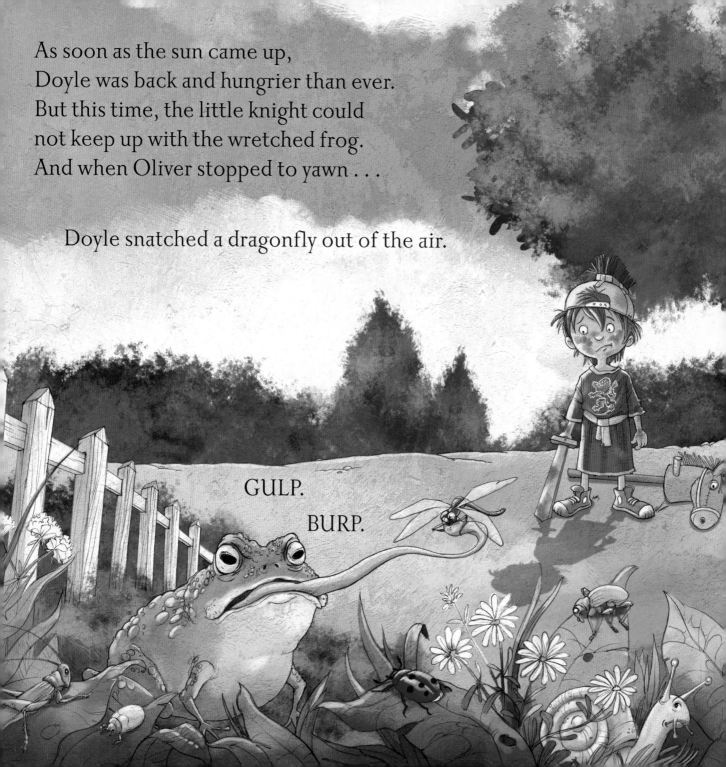

Sad and battle-worn, Oliver dragged himself inside.
He had lost, and his little bug friends were now
at the mercy of a very wicked frog.

"Mom, is the man in
the moon mean?"

Oliver was too afraid to even blink, which is why he saw the friendly, familiar light flickering outside his window.

"Good evening, Sir Oliver," the firefly said to his friend as he entered the room. "What was the trouble today?"

"Oh, Phineas, I'm so sorry! I–I'm too scared to close my eyes in the dark, and … and I was *sleepy*. That's why Doyle won today."

Oliver wiped away a tear.

"I wish God had given me a light like yours. Then I'd *never* be afraid of the dark."

"Oliver, everyone is afraid of something." Phineas glanced toward the window. "I'm scared of Doyle and the neighborhood children with their nets and jars. But everything you need is right here."

Oliver stared at the firefly, "What do you mean?"

"Well," Phineas began, "Psalm 91 says that those who live in the shelter of the Most High will find rest in the shadow of the Almighty."

"A shadow?!" Oliver frowned. "I could never rest in a creepy shadow."

"The *Almighty*, Oliver. That's God. The Bible says, 'He will cover you with His feathers; you will take refuge under His wings.' Just imagine it," Phineas said as he flitted toward the ceiling.

And stretching over Oliver's bed was the wing of a giant eagle—a feathery fortress, shielding Oliver from all the things that scared him.

"Wow, what else does it say?" Oliver said slowly, his eyes wide and fixed on the feathers.

"Verse 11 says, God will send His angels to protect you."
"Whoaaa!"

"You will defeat lions and cobras!
   You'll stomp on fierce serpents!"
   Oliver heard Phineas yell.

And the next thing he knew, Oliver was clutching the lion's mane and riding gallantly through the jungle, alongside a river, and into the wide open country side.

The little knight had
never felt more brave.

"You want to hear my favorite part?" Phineas asked his young friend. "The Lord says He will rescue those who love Him. He will protect those who trust Him. Whenever you call out to Him, He will answer. He will be with you."

"Good night, brave knight. Sunrise will be here soon, and along with it, the adventure you were created for. Tomorrow the battlefield will see a new day and a new knight."

"The one who lives under the protection of the Most High dwells in the shadow of the Almighty.
I will say to the LORD, 'My refuge and my fortress, my God, in whom I trust.'"

—Psalm 91:1-2

Remember:
[God] will cover you with His feathers; you will take refuge under His wings. His faithfulness will be a protective shield.—Psalm 91:4

Read:
Psalm 91:1–16. The Bible says that God is in charge, so we can feel safe. Sure, we'll still stump our toes, think bad thoughts, and get sick—we live in a broken world. But when we choose to trust Jesus, we're never alone, and God has a great adventure planned for our lives.

Think:
1. What scares Oliver?
2. What scares you?
3. Have you ever had to deal with a bully like Doyle? What happened?
4. Name a fear that has kept you from doing something you know you should do.
5. God is perfect. What about Him can you focus on when you are afraid?

Do:
Make your own protective wings.
1. Get two sheets of paper. Construction paper or cardstock is best, but any paper will do.
2. On each sheet of paper, draw (or ask an adult to draw) a large wing.
3. On one wing, write: "God will cover you with His feathers; you will take refuge under His wings." On the other wing, write: "God's faithfulness will be a shield."—Psalm 91:4
4. Cut out (or ask an adult to cut out) your wings. Color or decorate them.
5. Hang your wings over your bed, on the refrigerator, or by the door to remind you of God's protection. If you know someone else who is afraid, make them a set of wings too!

Long after your paper wings are gone,
God's wings of protection will still be there to shelter you.